Insubordinate

Raquel S. Downing

Legal & Disclaimer

The information contained in this book is not designed to replace or take the place of any form of medicine or professional medical advice. The information in this book has been provided for educational and entertainment purposes only.

The information contained in this book has been compiled from sources deemed reliable, and it is accurate to the best of the Author's knowledge; however, the Author cannot guarantee its accuracy and validity and cannot be held liable for any errors or omissions. Changes are periodically made to this book. You must consult your doctor or get professional medical advice before using any of the suggested remedies, techniques, or information in this book.

Upon using the information contained in this book, you agree to hold harmless the Author from and against any damages, costs, and expenses, including any legal fees potentially resulting from the application of any of the information provided by this guide. This disclaimer applies to any damages or injury caused by the use and application, whether directly or indirectly, of any advice or information presented, whether for breach of contract, tort, negligence, personal injury, criminal intent, or under any other cause of action.

You agree to accept all risks of using the information presented inside this book. You need to consult a professional medical practitioner in order to ensure you are both able and healthy enough to participate in this program.

Acknowledgments

&

Dedication

To my son! Thank you for allowing me to become the best mom possible. There is never a recipe for raising a child, but I am happy to be chosen to guide and direct you in living your best life.

To my parents! Dad, your long talks, lectures have allowed me to make some of the best critical decisions. Thank you. Mom, thank you for always being my greatest supporter and my best friend.

To my siblings! At the end of the day, there is nothing like having siblings to laugh, fight, and talk. I love each one of you.

To my friends! There is nothing like having good friends to motivate, support, and cherish forever.

I want every child to know that their voice can change the world, and using your voice to tell your story will always become history someday. For those who told me that I couldn't, this is why I did. Even when I am no longer here, my story will forever live and be told.

Author's Note

Sometimes, we experience things that we cannot share, and this makes us grow and develop, often in a unique way. When I was enrolled in Kindergarten, I could not explain my behavior to myself, my peers, and even my parents. It would not even have occurred to me that I "behaved" in a manner that might require explanation before others "got me." Thus, I had to dig in to become the little person I thought I had to be.

I believe the power is not in the tongue but in pen, and my dad instilled this idea in me long before today. So, I want to take this opportunity to use my pen and craft this book to let you into my life and understand no matter how huge the challenges came, I always landed on top, this is my story and this is my life.

In my life, I have been through trials and tribulations that many people have never even thought of. The way my parents, my mentors, and my community has helped me grow has made me the insubordinate and resilient person I am today.

I understand that there are certain reasons for everything that happens in life, be it good or bad. I believe we can always learn from our experiences; this way, we can make a difference.

I have fought a disparaging system and racism on multiple occasions. I am a woman who stands up for what is the right thing to do; I have done it for myself as well as for other people.

I believe people are supposed to help each other and be a helping hand for others. And we must stand up for the ones who cannot stand for themselves. I have seen people with abusive relationships, and I have been a victim to one myself.

I want to encourage people to stand up and fight, if not for others, at least for themselves. I reached my breaking point, but I ask you not to wait for your breaking point. When it is time to stand up, you know it, so you do it.

Always cherish your relationship; we have beautiful in our lives, but we start taking them for granted; please, don't take your love ones and everything else for granted. Let me tell you that wanting something and being given something are two different things, and we must realize this difference to understand the true value of what we have.

Through this book, I just want to let my heart out with you all, and it will be an honor for me if I can stir your soul and inspire you.

Contents

CHAPTER 1:

Raquel

If the temperament of a newborn is predicated on the weather conditions on the day she was born, the pleasant October morning Raquel Simone Downing saw her first light in the Maimonides Jewish Hospital - squeezed in between Borough Park, Crown Heights, and Prospect Heights, in Brooklyn, New York City - would predict that she would become a sweet girl with a quiet disposition.

As baby Raquel was on her way home, on the one hand, government teachers and transit workers were on strike on the streets. On the other hand, Irish and Italian gangs were fighting smaller neighborhood hoodlums to claim the control of Brooklyn's lucrative criminal underworld in the back alleys.

Brooklyn was also in an economic free-fall as it entered the 1960s. The naval dockyards closed down, and more than 12,000 workers were left unemployed. The U.S.

economy was floundering for the first time after the unstoppable boom that followed the end of the Second World War.

To make things worse, as the neighborhoods fell into despair, the ever-lurking infestation of racism reared its head in battle. As more and more African Americans moved in, the so-called "white flight" saw many whites move out to Long Island, which hastened the decay of the neighborhoods.

Well, Brooklyn was not always in such a tumultuous state; it all erupted when the New York Police shot to death an eleven-year-old black boy. The moment that ill-fated incident took place, Brooklyn went up in flames of protest, and race riots obliged the City to send in more than 1,000 police officers to quell the uprising.

People left in droves, and untold newcomers arrived. They brought a hodgepodge of exotic new cultures into the neighborhood. Eventually, everything fused in the trendy Brooklyn of today, driven along by a gentrification-funded renaissance.

On his way to the hospital, Raquel's beaming father would most likely pass Avenue P and East Second Street, where the old cultures of Brooklyn were still on display with a Chinese restaurant, a Kosher Butcher, and a pizzeria side by side. Again, he could just as likely have seen Bobby

Kennedy surrounded by hordes of black children posturing for the press or Steve Whitaker and Bill Robinson of the Yankees visiting the children in the Bedford-Stuyvesant neighborhood. The weekends brought festivity all around Brooklyn as people swarmed to the beaches of Coney Island and stood in line for hours and hours around Nathan's Hot Dog restaurant for one of New York's most revered meals.

In the same breath, the people of Brooklyn, irrespective of race and creed, often came together during tough times in a show of unity in pain. When two airliners collided in the fog above New York and crashed into the ground in Brooklyn's Park Slope neighborhood, everyone shared the emotional burden. The same happened when thousands and thousands of people lined on the streets of Brooklyn to show respect to the Italian-American mob boss and union leader, Anthony Anastasio. He was a part of the Gambino crime family that controlled the Brooklyn dockyards for more than 30 years.

On their way home after her birth, the family would have noticed sukkah structures being built all across Brownsville in preparation for the Jewish celebration of Sukkot. This festival follows shortly on the heels of Yom Kippur. On many street corners, men huddled around radios to listen to a broadcast of the Dodgers-Giants baseball game.

As the family drove neared home at sunset, hipsters expectantly lined up under the overhangs of the freeway on Third Avenue between 29th and 17th streets to watch muscle cars race madly down the public road unencumbered by any police presence.

It was really a very happening year in Brooklyn, and Raquel's life once again resonated with the situation in the borough in her adulthood. So, this was the America into which Raquel Simone Downing was delivered, and this is where her journey with many crests and troughs started.

CHAPTER 2:

Cambria Heights - Historic Black Community

Raquel's family resided in Cambria Heights, a historic black community with many well-known figures from different walks of life. A middle-class neighborhood, Cambria Heights was a close-knit community built on a trapezoid, cut from forest land and green pastures. The houses had larger lots than most of the surrounding areas like Nassau County to the east, Elmont, which was just beyond the Cross Island Parkway, and beyond Springfield Avenue to the West. The surrounding areas provided safe spaces for the children to play while adults intermingled with each other.

There little Raquel also enjoyed, and the older children loved playing with the cute little girl. Though everyone enjoyed her company, some girls found the opportunity to enjoy a little more☺. So, some girls, who wanted to get close to Raquel's brother, used her as an excuse. The bigger girls would collect Raquel at home and take her to their homes to do her hair or to the corner store for a sweet treat. For Raquel, life in Cambria Heights was like living in dream heaven.

Every black family in Cambria Heights was proud of the whole community; in fact, all families functioned like one large family. It didn't matter whether a family had an only child or a number of children to form their own soccer team; the whole neighborhood looked out for each other, always. This caring attitude pervaded throughout the community, and it indeed influenced Raquel's nature as she grew up.

Raquel's family was one of the largest families in the community. Still, Mr. Jones would take all of the children to the park to play baseball. Raquel still has the Louisville Slugger bat, which will always remind her of how daddy coached the boys' little league team after work.

She saw the men in the community volunteer to make sure that their boys and girls were never idle or engaged in any foul activities. Thus, they always remained around for better upbringing of every kid in the community. To stay busy with positive activities, Raquel took dancing and ballet classes and joined the girl scouts. Since she always had a great love for sports, she also ran track and played baseball, and it didn't matter that she was a girl. Of course, Raquel played with dolls too and made mud pies with friends in the backyard of her house. In the basement, they held concerts and sang to the earth, wind, and fire with their music group. One of the great things about Raquel is that she has a multifarious personality and can manage to deal with all kinds of activities. Thus, she never restricted herself from doing anything she wanted to, no matter if it was labeled for boys or girls. Till today, she carries her dynamic personality and lets it out gracefully.

Raquel always loves to recount her childhood memories fervently since her childhood life was tremendous. Also, she had the best friends one can ever wish to have; she still loves her childhood friends and has vivid memories of every moment they spent together. When all the kids gathered for fun, they enjoyed playing tag as their most favorite sport. Also, the boys and girls loved spinning the bottle - if you know what I mean. Oh God, those were the days, my friend. They all had great fun growing up.

Today, Cambria Heights is a nice community to live for whites and African Americans. You can find many local businesses in the vicinity where kids get the special attention they deserve. Parks and streets are clean, and it is safe to travel. However, it was not so peaceful and welcoming since the beginning. It was almost all-white enclave before the arrival of William H. Durham - the first black in Cambria Heights to face and survive against racism. Today, William H. Durham is known as the "Mayor of Cambria Heights." He stood his ground firmly and earned respect from white residents in the end that also cleared the entryway for other black families.

Cambria Heights was a middle-class black community, underestimated by most who lived there. In her childhood, Raquel never understood why their community remained under the radar in spite of producing some very prominent people who contributed to making New York City the most magnificent city in the world.

As she grew up and started her conscious educational years and profession, she came across the truth, which was always hidden in her plain sight. The witches and demons in the fairytale started appearing one after another, more dangerous than the previous one.

Life outside Cambria Heights was not what Raquel had imagined in her childhood. However, she had to meet the harsh realities. She could have been consumed by pessimism and negativity, but that WAS not so for Raquel. Yes, Cambria Heights had indeed prepared her for the challenges ahead to take head-on, and she did so successfully, even against the government organizations and departments.

CHAPTER 3:

The Prodigy

We don't often get to know and even listen to about prodigy kids. Being a prodigy is not usual, but again, being usual is not Raquel. She has been impressive all her life. She is a gifted one - the one way ahead of her time. She exhibited her talents in every phase of her life since her childhood. Today, she is a grownup, mature woman, but her talents seem to know no boundaries.

Raquel was a precocious child that tended to be somewhat serious, even cerebral. Still, she was gifted with a charisma that adults could neither ignore nor escape. It seemed as if young Raquel put a spell on the grownups. Whenever she entered the room, everyone felt obliged to shower her with affection. She could do no wrong and rarely did.

Crochet

Her gifted abilities started to show up when her paternal grandmother, Emma, took her favorite granddaughter to the TSS store to buy some yawn. Little Raquel was overpowered by the beautiful multi-colored yawn, and she was hooked right there.

When they arrived back home, the four-year-old solemnly joined the old ladies as they chatted amicably while threading their needles. In no time, Raquel amazed the old hands with her prodigious crocheting skills. Within a flash, the toddler was looping thread in and out, crocheting along and laughing at the little jokes, even those she did not fully understand yet.

"No one ever saw something like it." Years later, her grandmother said. "A natural. She was a natural."

It seemed at the time, long before the strength of Raquel's desire to succeed and rise to the top, became known to everyone who knew her.

Commerce

Raquel was also gifted in matters of commerce. The young go-getter started a summer internship at Citibank, straight from school, with no clue of how immensely talented she was in commerce and numbers. It became impossible for her superiors to let her go at the end of her internship.

Thus, the mere internship quickly turned into a permanent job as they discovered her splendid gift for numbers. She quickly learned how to manage petty cash and run payroll. At the tender age of seventeen, the young black woman was running the numbers for Citibank at 399 Park Avenue in the finance department.

Later, at the Seaman's Savings Bank, she quickly became the number one teller. When she joined the New York Mercantile Exchange as a Computer Operator, she learned how to trade in commodities, stocks, crude oil, and sugar at the speed of lighting. Very tough job she was responsible of putting in those trades in a matter of seconds.

A Keen Observer

It is said that our talents attract us to the careers we follow. Unhappiness overcomes us when we are prevented from developing our abilities in our choice of a job. In Raquel's case, she was destined for a career in medicine. Her talent for observation served her empathetic nature. Since she has a very goal-oriented personality, this translates into a burning desire to make life better for those around her. This is who she had always been; even way back when she first thought something was not right with her baby brother.

When she sensed that something was not right with her baby brother, she went back into the nursery and watched him as he breathed softly and frowned and wrinkled nose in the effort. Indeed, his hands were unnaturally clammy, almost moist. In a flash of insight, she saw it clearly now. Clammy hands. Ashen little hands. That was not right. Something was wrong with her darling little brother. Raquel's observation was perfect, but unfortunately, no one understood her talent of observation at that time. As a result, the family had to suffer from an irreversible loss.

On another occasion, Raquel was there to save mom's life. Her mother was having a stroke while Raquel was there, so she immediately took her mom to the hospital. There she was, standing in front of four physicians. Before they could diagnose, Raquel told them that her mother was having a stroke, which they later confirmed. Thus, the physicians rushed to treat her mom to another hospital specializing in treating stroke and had to perform quickly for her mother to have a fighting chance of making a full recovery. Witnessing her amazing observation ability, the whole team of doctors became more interested in knowing who Raquel was. Was she a doctor herself?

Multitasker

It is very usual for individuals to follow a single career path and perform very well and go on adding many feathers in their caps. Indeed, it is usual, but the word "usual" doesn't exist in Raquel's dictionary. Unique is Raquel that makes her a powerhouse of multiple talents; she can manage multiple tasks at the same time, and that too flawlessly.

CHAPTER 4

That Girl Who Everyone Loved

Raquel has always had a mesmerizing persona that attracts everyone she meets and greets, including her family members, teachers, and friends.

Mom's Angel

"She was a naturally sweet girl." Those that knew her all say without any reservation. "She was her momma's little girl, and she clung to her mom like a shadow."

Wherever her Mom went, Raquel followed. She was a quiet girl, and she had the scientist's temperament from day one. She would observe her parents, her siblings, and family friends quietly but intently, and absorbed everything.

After watching her Mom, she would subtly move in and start handing her things when she cooked and cleaned. In no time there she was, Raquel, the assistant working the kitchen and the bedrooms in step with her Mom, cooking, cleaning, and serving supper to the family as if she had been doing it for years and years.

Motherly Instincts

Raquel's role in the family is significant, and she is ever ready to help her family members. The Downing's was a large bustling family, and there were always younger ones that needed to be watched. At the same time, the mother was multi-tasking somewhere else in the household. Within no time, Raquel was taking care of this as well. Whenever the younger siblings wanted to play outside, Raquel magically appeared like a guardian angel, well versed in toddler care as she observed her mother's moves all her life.

She was a natural in more than just crocheting and numbers. She had natural nurturing instincts, which became evident from a very early age. While many young girls are attracted to babies and like to help their moms to feed and take care of the baby, Raquel took nurturing to new levels. She was all-in and involved in every part of caring for her baby brother. Raquel never lost interest or slacked off. Later on, it was natural for her to become a nurturing mom too.

The Sweetheart

She was very popular amongst the grown-ups too. Every so often, her Mom's friends would take her along when they went shopping, and they competed to babysit her. The adults loved spoiling her, and Raquel responded with quiet charm. She was a beautiful little girl and remunerated those who treated her with sweetness and warmth. Raquel never had to ask for anything. Whatever she desired was readily available from the hands of those who adored her.

Sometimes Aunt Dancy, who lived nearby, would come around and pick her up. She loved doing Raquel's hair and often brought her back sporting a flashy mature hairstyle that Raquel's Dad found inappropriate for his baby girl.

Dancy's daughter, Mila, quickly understood that her Mom, and her Dad, Jacob, never refused Raquel anything. Pretty soon, sweet Raquel became her and Raquel's sister's envoy to ask for stuff they wanted.

The Pretzel Model

When Raquel entered first grade, she focused all of her displaced emotions on her teacher. Mrs. Harvey adored Raquel and nurtured her, and in return, Raquel grew very attached to that well-dressed and very professional lady.

It was no secret that Raquel was her favorite. She made Raquel the "pretzel model" for the class and often slipped her an extra pretzel when no one looked. In Mrs. Harvey's class, Raquel was never off the radar and never invisible. As a result, Raquel opened up and returned the affection. It was a healthy antidote to her attempts at home to become invisible.

Seeing how Raquel embraced the attention, the warm-hearted teacher always called on Raquel first. Ms. Harvey was an example of professionalism in the workplace. When Raquel became a teacher, she always strove to be as professional as Mrs. Harvey.

It was not all Mrs. Harvey's doing, though. Raquel had charisma, and when she received attention, she responded with a warm sweetness that drew people closer to her.

Big-Eyed Girl

A woman's eyes are the windows to her soul. In literature, men often describe falling in love with a woman's eyes. Men love a woman with enormous, almost childlike eyes. Little Raquel was a girl with huge and gorgeous eyes. As she went through puberty, the boys began to notice the pretty girl with the seductive eyes. Raquel was oblivious until the least talkative boy in the class - the boy who literally never said anything - remarked how beautiful her eyes were.

Raquel: *"Why do you like my eyes?" she responded, trying not to appear coy.*

Darius: *"I don't know," Darius stammered, a bit taken aback. "They're pretty," he mumbled.*

Raquel looked up at him with those eyes and gave him her sexiest "Kool-Aid" smile. She wanted to say a lot more but was too scared to express what she felt, although she always thought that no one cared how she felt.

When one of the adults also commented on "how gorgeous" her eyes were, she started to take note, although she was quite perturbed at first.

Raquel was in love with Darius, and she thinks Darius was also in love with her. Raquel is a warm and sensual woman who has such a lot of love to give. She seems to be a woman that will marry her soul mate.

Raquel wanted to tell Darius things, a lot of things, but she didn't want to scare him away. "If only Darius opened up," she sighs. It's the eternal question - what do women want, why can't men talk about it? Has it always been like that?

Raquel says she often feels like she's in a love story, not a tragedy, thankfully.

> *"So, I'm in a love story, and - it's like the*
> *Truman Show, you know - and I am the only*
> *one with absolutely no idea what's going on."*

Always a Giver, Not a Taker

Many would say that Raquel "Really? She has a good heart, they'll say. Raquel laughs deeply and adds, "I hope. I always give. Possessions. Time. Support. What have you? I believe that I am used as a vessel to help others in life. Raquel's laugh is one of a kind, and her smile can light up the world.

When I celebrated a new chapter in life, I had a massive party at my house. Everyone had to write down a defining memory they had of me.

One friend wrote:

> *"It was you who made me travel. You are a*
> *traveler - to Egypt, Dubai, London, Belize,*
> *Turkey, Russia, and France. Now I am a*
> *traveler too. Thank you, Raquel."*

Another friend wrote:

> *"Raquel, we met through an acquaintance,*
> *and you never forgot me. We have been*
> *friends ever since."*

Hannah reminisced about their first meeting:

> *"It was during our orientation at PSCH, and I knew from day one that you were a go-getter. You were ambitious, and oh my God, how determined you were."*

Raquel's friends all describe her as an exciting person. One friend described her as fun:

> *"She dances the night away when we go out, but she can be very entertaining at home too. She is a very social person, and she never stops dancing - the salsa especially, the girl, has the moves."*

But then, she goes to the gym religiously. Many of the girls here love to Google Raquel. They always find something, a little nibble, to fuel their gossip behind her back. The funny thing is that Raquel sees it all.

Kool-Aid

Raquel's one nickname, Kool-Aid, comes from her smile, according to her friends who described her smile as a brilliant "Kool-Aid" smile that can melt even the coldest hearts. When she was a bit older, Raquel gave herself a pseudonym, and her choice provides a little bit of insight into how the budding woman wanted to define herself.

It is undoubtedly "cool" if your girlfriends called you "Kool-Aid," but Raquel preferred her other nickname.

When she was smaller, her friends put the diminutive Rocky forward instead of Raquel (little Raquel), and the name stuck. Some called her Brainy, and she never understood why.

When she entered her teenage years, and the girls made their own sweatshirts, Raquel printed the name "Rocky" on the back of her shirt. Later on, when the rapping craze hit the girls, she changed her sweatshirt. Now it said "Raquel" on the front and "Rockwell" on the back. She made a choice to be reliable (solid as a rock) instead of pursuing the "cool" identity that her friends already bestowed on her. This preference would also be reflected by her choices later in life.

Lucky in Romance too?

As a young woman, Raquel yearned for love. Today, a mature woman, Raquel, is still single, but she is not cynical. Raquel still believes in love at first sight, but by now, she believes even more in tough love. Action speaks louder than words. Experience taught me to ignore unwarranted behavior, but not to disregard it. At the same time, she doesn't believe that chivalry is dead, and she really thinks that she has true love in her near future. DRUM ROLL PLEASE

True love? Her parents always wanted it for her. She knows her Dad really wants to walk her down the aisle and give her away. She prays that she will get married while her Mom and Dad are still around. They really want to see her wedding. They desperately want the best of everything for her.

Raquel's Dad told her a few weeks ago that she needed to start working on finding a husband. He never said anything like this to her before. Not even close. He wants her to hear his voice. She knows he wants her to be taken care of when he is no longer there for her. It disturbs him that she hasn't found the right husband yet - someone who will step up when he passes away, someone to protect and provide for her.

Raquel's Dad was the very first man she ever loved. She still does - as much. She was engaged once, but it didn't work out. She learned a lot from experience; she learned to focus on herself and to put God first. Only if God comes first will she be able to recognize the right man when God sends him to her.

As for Dwight, she isn't proud of that episode in her life. Looking back, she can see how unhealthy it was. She had to really go on her knees before God and pray for Him to open her eyes. Without Him, she couldn't break free. Through prayer, eventually, He revealed to her that it was now the time to break free.

So, Granny said to her, "Don't you be no fool for no man. She said it right to her face. "I don't think Dwight is right for you. I really don't; he is not the one. What's the matter with you, girl?" She came on strong. Did she make the wrong choice? She didn't know about that. All she knew was that she was desperately unhappy."

She could not admit to anyone, even herself, that she was in an abusive relationship. She was the level-headed one. She was an intelligent girl with mind-blowing mathematical talents and filled to the brim with emotional intelligence. She is not that girl. She couldn't be. So, she refused to listen to anyone, even to her own voice. She just blanked it all out to make it possible to stay with Dwight.

When Dwight insisted that they get married, she was elated. She thought this was as good as it got. The good and the bad - both go into true love, so she believed. And of course, she said yes - she was deliriously happy - elated. But she was wrong, of course. Very wrong.

The Ring, perhaps it was all in the Ring. Many thought, wow, that's a gorgeous ring. People would say he must love you. I was amazed that a ring holds so much value rather than the focus of a healthy relationship. A month before the wedding, Raquel caught him.

He was a cheat. He was a philanderer. And yes, he abused her physically and hurt her badly.

Anyone could be in her shoes at this moment. A Woman, A Man, A Girl Or A Boy. Raquel knew all too well that this wasn't a healthy relationship.

According to her doctor, her labs do not fit a diagnosis of what she is going through, but something causes her symptoms. She knows that the physical abuse in her past, but her lips remain sealed. It is hard to talk about it. She is a bit vain in that sense – she doesn't want people to know that she – she – succumbed to an abusive man and suffered so much in an abusive relationship. Thank goodness I could see that this wasn't something that I wanted to be part of. This is not what I know to be a healthy relationship.

That there is more that I look for in a man, but getting to know myself first is the recipe of who I am as a person, and then I would be able to allow someone into my life. Forgiveness is the key to be able to move on. So, she moved on. She sees everything in a different light now. She now sees love as something that comes from inside of you. She loves *Corinthians 13:4-7*, and she recites from memory:

> *"Love is patient, Love is kind. It does not envy, it does not boast, it is not proud. It is not rude, it is not self-seeking, it is not easily angered, it keeps no record of wrongs. Love does not delight in evil but rejoices with the truth."*

Raquel changed after that. She now prays every day, she meditates, and she never ponders over what strangers might think of her. She puts God first in her life, for sure, and she is kind of immune to how they treat her. She doesn't really care about all that.

And she still believes that it will come when it is time. As the Bible says, *love is patient*. And so is she.

CHAPTER 5:

The Downing Family

The Downing family dynamics are rich socially, financially, and culturally. The ancestors made great progression and established the family well. The Downing family does not have roots in slavery as far as they know. Research and census records show that their ancestors come from the Caribbean Islands of Barbados, where they originated from Nigeria to parts of South Carolina and Virginia. The latter inhabited the island for the last 1000 years. The family was known to be the best engineers on the island, and they were revered as boat builders. Those that eventually reached the shores of the United States became sharecroppers. This is where Raquel's grandfather, a white man in the deep south, met and married his wife, a black southerner who became Raquel's great-great-grandmother.

Fastidious living and careful planning lifted the sharecroppers up from the breadline, and they eventually became wealthy southern landowners and commercial farmers. Raquel's father was born into a privileged and prosperous family. Life was good; grandfather had twelve siblings, and grandmother had eleven. Many believe that a family's wealth is measured by their numbers, and this was certainly the case for this family.

It might come as a surprise to many people that a black family can have a heritage in the American Dream, but the Downing family has had its fair share in the American Dream. Still, not all black families come from slavery, and not all blacks see themselves as victims, and as such, purely the result of "white mastery."

The Downing ancestors were successful and independent people who flourished as entrepreneurs long before the civil rights movement. On her mother's side, Raquel comes from a long line of real estate investors. They made a vast fortune from horse racing, the sport of kings, which they invested in their sprawling real estate portfolio.

The family was close to their elders, who were directly involved in raising the children. They imparted wisdom and a love of horses to their grandchildren and lived to a ripe old age. Even now, when Raquel talks about them, her tears well-up.

DAD, YOU ARE THE BEST!

Raquel's father has always been a "real man." He is known for his deep conversation, and you better be paying attention to him. He is the classical strong and silent type. He never shows emotion if it represents any form of weakness. He was always strong for his family.

In those troubling times, in the valley of death, Raquel's innate sense of detail and empathetic connection with those around her allowed her to see beyond her Dad's silent facade. Inside, he was a dead-man-walking, but he never confided in anyone, and he never lost face. He suffered in agonizing silence, all alone. Except for Raquel, who saw it, and sensed it, and never let on.

She watched him in awe, day after day. At the same time, her Mom was true to her feminine role and cried and shared her pain and allowed others to see her suffer, but her Dad had to carry his cross all alone. Her admiration was coupled with a deep comprehension of the "slings and arrows" of masculine experience. She developed a level of wisdom that belied her age.

Her Dad is a superman - the real superman, and from him, she drew her own strength and her quiet personal courage during testing times. She was, no doubt about it, also her Dad's little girl, and the two of them shared an unspoken bond ever since.

Guardian Grannies

Her attachment to both her grandmothers never wavered. Over the years, they just grew closer, and Raquel cared for them until the very end. During the holidays, both grandmothers stayed with Raquel and her family. It was Raquel who took them to the doctor and to shopping, and it was again Raquel who paid their bills on time.

Adella

Adella is Raquel's maternal grandmother. Today, Raquel can see the resemblance she shows to her grandmother Adella. Like Raquel, she lived for others. When her neighbors were happy, she was, and the rest of the time, she doted on her own family. She shared her passions with them, her appreciation of music, and her love of life, good food, and cooking. Her macaroni cheese and collard greens were legendary; today, Raquel has taken over this role in the family. Whenever a cookout is planned, everyone turns to Raquel, who does not have to take a backseat when it comes to macaroni cheese and collard greens.

She left the Deep South and made her way up to New York to make a better life for herself. Here she met and married Raquel's grandfather, and together they conquered the world. It is interesting to point out that both her grandfathers and grandmothers were smart and conservative with money; they always invested wisely and lived frugally, so they soon became financially secure.

Adella and her husband owned properties from Brooklyn to Sag Harbor. They owned homes in Sag Harbor, one of Long Island's most exclusive neighborhoods, as well as numerous brownstones in Clinton Hills, Park Slope, and Bedford Stuyvesant.

On her deathbed, grandmother Adella was worried only about one thing: how people will treat Raquel after she was gone. "Don't allow any man to make a fool of you, my dear child." Grandmother Adella warned Raquel.

Emma

From her paternal side, Raquel was exposed to a grandmother that was way ahead of her times. She was an educated and health-conscious woman who ate clean and never wasted food. As a qualified nutritionist, she could back her advice up with rational explanations and evidence. She understood the connection between nutrition and disease before mainstream science did.

Frugality ran through her veins despite her wealth. Up to the day she died, she cut coupons from magazines to purchase her list at a discount; thus, after shopping for her needs, she would always have money left. She taught Raquel that only poor people waste money, whereas rich people were too intelligent to spend wildly, and it did not end there. She always insisted on using money orders when she paid her bills. This, she explained, made it impossible for the crooks to "steal your identity." And she exposed Raquel to the philosophy of "baby-steps." Save one or two dollars every single day, and pretty soon, you will sit on a fortune. Raquel grabbed and applied this idea to all facets of her life. Thus, by doing her small bit every day, she graduated from multiple universities in multiple fields - every day, a baby step.

Raquel had a tough time letting go. When the end came for grandmother, Emma, Raquel begged her not to go. Her grandmother knew better. "You'll be just fine, dear. I'm ready to get out of here."

My Son

"I prayed all the time. I was petrified. I knew I had to be strong, for him, and for myself. So I prayed, and I went back to school." I will never forget when my son called me and said that he was asleep and bit his tongue. I knew that he immediately had to go to the hospital. I told him to go and call me afterward. I kept calling him, waiting for him to respond. No answer. I contacted that special number that the military gives for an emergency to family members. The worst I had ever felt in my entire life. I got the call from the hospital, and the Surgeon and the military immediately rushed me to get myself ready because I was needed to report to my son. He has cancer. What a blow! If I can say how alone I was, this was it. My son was diagnosed with Cancer. He had a huge, malignant tumor inside his head.

> *Raquel recounts: "I remember my son calling me to tell me that he was about to jump from a helicopter. My heart skipped a beat, but I couldn't say anything other than to ask him to pray and to remember everything they taught him to make a safe landing. He did! My son called me afterward to let me know that he was okay."*

> *Raquel says: "I raised a real man. He is a hero, a soldier, a husband, and a father. He served his country, and he serves God. Not bad for a single mom, hey? Not that I brought him into the world physically, but God loaned my son to me to raise him to become this and everything else that he is supposed to grow into on this earth."*

Oldest Brother

The oldest brother, as a child, used to get all siblings up so that they could go and run on the track with him. They used to come home with all the trophies. They were all torn, but Raquel believes that her oldest brother was affected most because they were very close.

Older Sister

Raquel's sister has always been a tough girl, while Raquel was a bit passive when compared with her sister's attitude toward life. Just like Raquel was there for others, her sister was there for Raquel, so she wouldn't let anyone bother Raquel. Because Raquel was quiet, her sister felt that she needed to protect her from those who thought that they could push over Raquel. The sisters did everything together as children; however, they didn't like it when mom would dress them up with the same outfits in different colors.

Raquel's sister was smart and did not have to study for anything; she could take a test and pass easily, whereas Raquel learned everything, but she always had to work harder to study. Always felt nervous about taking tests.

CHAPTER 6:

Tragedies Strike!

No one fully understands the formation of a young mind, and no theory offers an explanation of how childhood events shape us and drive our future development. Nevertheless, we become because of the trauma and tribulations and the love and beauty we encounter on our way to adulthood. For Raquel, this was even more so. Raquel's journey so far has not been without miseries and tragedies. She has endured deaths and diseases of her close relations and legal trials and tribulations.

Farewell, My Baby Brother

Raquel spun around and stormed into the pantry; where her Mom was leaning against a small ladder trying to reach a can of soup on the top shelve.

"Mom, something is wrong with…"

Her Mom almost lost her balance and frowned down at her little girl, who very rarely raised her voice. She showed some irritation, which she tried to hide from the sensitive girl. She sighed, audibly, but nevertheless followed her extraordinary little girl down the hall to the nursery.

After Raquel explained the symptoms three times, her Mom still shook her head and frowned. "I'm sorry, dear. I just don't see it. Do you mean he is too pale? He looks fine to me!"

Raquel looked at her baby brother, and then at her Mom. Maybe she was wrong, but his hands were sweating and seemed - different. She had to let it go. Mom smiled at her, stroked her hair, and kissed her. "Now, quickly, ask your dad if he wants coffee."

Raquel woke up with a sense of dread. She shuddered, sitting up, trying to figure out what she heard. It was her baby brother, gasping for air, groaning from discomfort, wheezing in an attempt to get daddy to make the suffocation go away. She shrieked and ran around the corner and down the little steps to the nursery where the lights were shining, and her Mom was crying, holding her hair away from her face as if it could burn her cheeks.

Raquel shuffled around her Mom and froze. Her Dad, looking bewildered, was bending next the cot and performing CPR on his boy's infantile little chest. Raquel never saw anyone doing CPR before, but she instinctively grasped the fact that Dad was trying to make her little baby brother alive again. Every now and then, she would stare at her Mom, her eyes trying to say, "I told you so," but her Mom was preoccupied with her son's wellbeing only.

When the emergency services arrived, the boy was breathing again. Her Dad nearly collapsed from aftershock as the ambulance rushed away noisily. The well-wishing neighbors quickly dispersed as Mom and Dad rushed to the station wagon to follow the ambulance.

When her kid brother left the house, he was still alive. It would be the last time Raquel would ever see him. By the next morning, he was dead, and the erstwhile bustling Downing's would never, ever be the same again.

The darkness that enveloped the family after the baby's death was compounded by their sense that they lost their little son twice in one night. First off, the trauma of trying to keep him alive until the paramedics arrived. Then the cataclysmic relief after the hospital informed Mr. and Mrs. Downing that their baby made it. He is safe, and he is now sleeping comfortably," - and the zinger - "All is well now, please, go home and get some sleep. You will see your little boy tomorrow morning. He'll be fine!"

It touched Raquel and her family deeply. She could not believe that, while she was having ice cream with her siblings and joking and playing after Dad told them the baby was alive and well, the angel of death came for him and took him to Jesus. Somehow, she did not think that her brother would have wanted to leave them all to go to Jesus yet. She discovered a new emotion, inconsolable grief, and she never forgot it.

The infant's death did not break her parents. Eighty percent of parents who lose a child separate and divorce, but they stayed together. It did change them, however. No one would ever be the same after that.

Up to his dying day, her father was wracked with a sense of guilt. He should never have left his boy that night; he would repeat whenever the subject came up. He should have been there for him.

Deep in his heart of hearts, her father suspected some malfeasance. "It was just too strange, too coincidental," he muttered. "Why would the hospital tell them the baby was healthy and fully recovered, and admonish them to leave and go home, if the baby was still critical? Or was it their fault the baby died? Did they do something wrong? Were they responsible?" Those were the questions in life that could never be answered; they are dragged along by the generations that follow as time goes by.

"I should never have left." That is all that remains vivid for Raquel. She was programmed to never make the same mistake in her life.

She was also burdened by the fact that she warned her mother that the baby was ill. She was also aware of the guilt and pain her parents carried around. They struggled with regrets every single day. So, Raquel dedicated herself to always doing the right thing, no matter what the cost.

Dear Brother, we'll always miss you.

Families absorb tragedy in unique ways, which are often invisible to outsiders. As strange as it is, life goes on, and no matter who goes off into the yonder, those who stay behind get up and get on, no matter what happened. The Downing family was no exception. Everything changed, but somehow everything seemed to remain the same. There was still joy, but it was no longer unqualified and ignorant of the pain and sadness that were left behind in the crevasses of their memories.

Summer camp offered the family the opportunity to embrace the changing of the seasons from dark and cold and sad to bright, vivacious, optimistic, and new beginning for a survivor family. Hope was back in the air, albeit very gingerly at first. It was hard coping with the feeling of guilt if you enjoyed yourself while your dear little brother was dead and gone.

Both of Raquel's brothers were booked for the camp, but her third oldest brother lost his place since her second oldest brother wanted to go camping. Her second oldest brother went camping, and the third oldest did not attend because he did not want to go. Nevertheless, her parents gave them ample space to make their own choices, so her second oldest was the only one who went to summer camp. However, their parents laid down many rules and conditions before he could go. No one blamed their parents for tending toward overprotection at this point in time. It was understood since the rules were made for good measure. As they knew, accidents happen - so rule number one was "absolutely no swimming" and "absolutely never, ever, go on the water."

Her second oldest brother could not swim; he was a bit scared of the water, and he was the only one of them who wore glasses, without which he had great difficulty seeing. Since this was summer camp, after all, the Downing parents set a premium precondition to the camp administration, something even the camp goers were made aware of. In essence, it was reflected in the parents' agreement they had to undersign before her second oldest brother could go - he meant no-water. Everyone agreed. Period.

"At least we would not get a call in the middle of the night, saying he drowned," her Dad said drily. He was clearly feeling a bit guilty for keeping him away from all the watersports all summer.

It started with a phone call. It was the camp director, and he urgently needed them to come. This was upsetting, but no one expected it to be this catastrophic. Her parents waited all night. It was an apologetic but insistent ringing of the front doorbell after eleven at night. Only the kitchen light was still on, and everyone was asleep except Mom. She enjoyed her only private moment of the day with a cup of coffee before retiring to bed.

Mom got up, but she had a premonition, and her legs gave away, and she screamed for Dad, who ran to the kitchen and helped her up. They heard the ringing again, more insistent, even more apologetic at the same time, and together they opened the door. Both of them cried when the man took his hat off and tried to speak.

They just knew that her second oldest brother was dead. The crying brought the neighbors of this typically quiet neighborhood out. Crying for the dead is unique, and people instinctively recognize it. They understood something tragic happened, and they came to see what happened. The Downing family lived in a close-knit community in Cambria Heights, and people from all over tried to console all of them. It was a terrible shock to the community. Most parents had children attending Kiwanis

Club Camp. Her second oldest brother, who at the age of thirteen, was almost six feet tall, was a humble boy everyone liked, and he was now departed, a loss for the entire community.

Tragedies happen when a series of unlikely coincidences strike at the same time. For her second oldest brother, things just fell apart. He should never have been on the water. He was on the water because the supervisor was unfamiliar with the condition his parents emphasized in the camp agreement.

He was in a canoe on the lake with a group of boys. One of his companions in the boat was the one boy who had incessantly bullied him and should have been placed in another group. But he wasn't.

He was wearing a life jacket, which should have been adequately checked for being perfectly functional by a supervisor. But it wasn't tested, and it wasn't properly fitted. So, that life-jacket could not save his life after he fell into the lake.

There should have been a responsible adult or camp leader in the canoe with the boys for discipline and to keep the boys safe, but there wasn't. The boys were left to their own devices, and as had been said so many times after havoc struck - boys will be boys. On this day, the boys were boys, and one died in the attempt.

On open water, you should behave yourself and not endanger other people. On this day, the bully could not stop harassing her second oldest brother. In the end, a scuffle developed, and her brother died in the water.

When a group of boys is taken onto open water in a canoe, it is tantamount on the adults in charge to provide lifesavers nearby for emergencies. No child should be left all alone in a boat on the lake without safety precautions, but on that day, no one showed up to be the adult in the room. The boys desperately tried to save him from the dark waters of the lake. Still, they lacked the skills and the strength and were subsequently severely traumatized too.

As a result of all these coincidental errors, he became the second boy from the Downing family to suffocate - and die - in less than one year. It was a travesty beyond the perception of any bystander.

While the guilt borne by Raquel's Mom and Dad after the death of the baby was subdued and implicit, they suffered severe feelings of profound guilt because of the postcard.

After the camp director paid his respects and said all the perfunctory things he had to say in his situation, he bid us farewell and left. No one actually remembers him going. He was just not there anymore, later on.

Raquel avidly watched Glen Ford's popular television show called "When Havoc Struck" in the late 1970s. It had titles like "When Havoc Struck, Bridge collapse" or "When Havoc Struck, Volcano," so she had an uncanny comprehension of what it meant when "havoc struck."

For the Downing family, this was "when havoc struck." Time stood still, and everyone numbed down to the lowest level of terrible sadness and regret. Nothing else mattered; nothing remained but the pain.

The postcard from her second oldest brother that arrived earlier on the same day the Camp Director visited us, remained on the mantle, and no one "dared to speak its name." Just a few hours ago, the family was drinking tea and eating little southern buttermilk biscuits. At the same time, Mom read his postcard out loud. Everyone laughed and joked until he espoused on his planned trip in a canoe on the lake the very afternoon, at the precise moment they enjoyed their tea and buttermilk biscuits. Afterward, this left everyone dead inside and far removed from the pleasures of life.

Still, despite the tea and biscuits, everyone quieted down. Dad looked at Mom in surprise, and the kids looked at each other and then at their parents in anticipation.

Dad turned to Mom shaking his head vehemently. "Surely, mother, he knows he is not allowed on the water, doesn't he?"

"Mom nodded in agreement, and then, true to form, to keep everyone calm, she continued, "I suppose he would be all right, wouldn't he?"

Dad nodded, but not without hesitation. "You think? I suppose so." He slurped his tea and spilled some, and Mom got up and dried his jacket.

"By the grace of God," Mom muttered, and everyone assumed that was it. One more coincidence. One more needle pressed into the flesh of the parents who brought us into the world and so often battled with regrets afterward.

Looking back, these were pivotal moments in the development of the Raquel Downing we know today. Here she saw with her own eyes how patient care and family interests are mismanaged by hospital administrations that are focused on different priorities.

If the family had a Patient Advocate or representative, maybe they would not have left, and perhaps the baby would still be alive today. If they had a health advocate, perhaps they would have had greater clarity over what happened at the hospital after they both left.

The family's wretchedness was aggravated by their failure to do anything to stop her second oldest brother from going ahead. But they did nothing besides having tea. If they had a family advocate at the time, it might have alleviated their distress.

The more we see of death, the less we see of life. This was not the case for Raquel. Instead, she started to see more and developed more empathy; she now felt more pain for more people. No doubt, this started her on the career path she now follows.

I See You, Brother!

When a loved one dies, they are taken from us, but their spirit often stays behind. Raquel, despite her inner strength, suffered quietly. She became very fearful of the dark. She absolutely refused to go to bed if the lights could not remain on.

The family home became a place of doom and gloom. Wherever Raquel went inside the house, they were there. She could not stop the longing. Everyone in the family had their specific spaces. At the dining room table, his chair was right next to their Dad's chair and now served as a stark reminder of his absence. It remained "his chair" even after he died.

In the living room, every sibling had a specific preferred and reserved place on the carpet where they could stretch out to watch their favorite television shows. No one ever took somebody else's spot. After death invaded the house, Raquel could not watch television anymore. The empty spots on the carpet reminded her too much of the sadness that she was trying to escape. In her mind, the spaces they used to occupy in the family home became sacred spaces where they would always remain.

Dread now filled an empty house where laughter used to conquer all else, and the silence communicated their profound suffering. Raquel became anxious and withdrawn, and after her second oldest brother death, she started to walk in her sleep. Many nights her parents found her fast asleep, going downstairs and walking toward the front door. They left her alone, allowed her to keep walking while they watched over her until she woke up. Siblings are just as affected by the death of a child in the home as their parents are, and Raquel was no exception - she was severely traumatized by his death, and she came a very long way after that up to the time she prepared for the departure of her grandparents.

In the aftermath of her second oldest brother's death, her parents understood that they needed to remove her from the toxic environment. She was sent off for a prolonged stay with family and friends to allow her to clear her mind and move on with her own life. This saved Raquel and brought her back from the dark, brooding place where she almost buried herself. But the brothers remained present in the life of the family.

Thinking and experiencing your own mortality at Raquel's age did not leave her perception of the world around her, unaffected. Raquel grappled with life and death, time and space, and body and soul to figure out where her brothers went after they died. She did not understand death as the end of things but as a change of address for the soul.

Everything reminded them of him. There were his sneakers, which he wore when he drowned; they became a constant reminder of his absence. And the regrets, "why did I not visit him just one more time before he died?"

Raquel had a vivid memory of the beautiful white casket and the white suit he wore. She just could not quite understand why he did not move at all. Was he asleep?

And she always lamented: how did all of this happen? How did we get from happiness to this? A week ago, we were all running around, having a great time at the big picnic. We got so tired we never even said proper goodbyes. No one knew that would be the last time they played with their second oldest brother.

After his death, the family often sensed his presence around the house. The spot where they played their games and the special place they laid down to watch television, even Raquel's memories of how she would moan and groan when he moved his feet too close to her face, were stark reminders of his absence.

After he died, the family often thought they heard him sliding down the rails again, using his feet to propel him down in a flash. No one else ever made that specific sounds coming downstairs. And that was not all. Every year on the anniversary of her second eldest death, the house somehow smelled like the salty seawater does at the lake.

In Ashes

Everyone pitied them, but their agony resulted in a few positives too. It heightened Raquel's sense of awareness due to the stress-induced fight-or-flight response. Soon she became even more attentive to the needs of others, especially her mother, who became very frail after the loss of two of her boys in one year. Raquel plainly refused to leave her mother alone for even one minute.

When her Mom turned around, there she was.

When her Mom woke up, there she was.

When her Mom went out, there she was.

Her presence calmed her Mom, but she had no idea that her daughter knew that she was unlikely to survive the grief without support. Raquel did not hesitate. For her, it was only natural. Those who are strong take care of those who are weak. That is how she saw life from very early on and still does.

CHAPTER 7:

Resilience

———— ༄ ༅ ༄ ————

Reflecting on her brother's death, she often felt a deep sadness. She never understood why her brother got into the canoe. Why? He knew he was not allowed to go on the water. He knew he would drown if they capsized. He knew the bully was on the boat, sitting right behind him. He knew his parents told him to avoid going anywhere near the water. "But the other part also knows that if an adult says to go, they go. I'm sure that is what happened to my brother. So why, in the name of God, did he do wrong when he knew what the right thing was to do?" Wonders Raquel.

She struggled with her parent's passivity too. Surely, she thought, they should have taken instant action after reading the postcard. Could they not have phoned the camp to end it all before it was too late? It wouldn't have mattered. The postcard came the same day that our beloved brother died.

She took these lessons to heart. Her conclusion was to always endeavor to do the right thing, no matter how hard it was. By then, she was already cast in stone.

This was the insight that made her refuse to get off the bus at the wrong destination and, much later on, made her stand up to the powers behind New York City's Department of Education.

It was a long journey for a five-year-old, but Raquel had to take the bus every morning to her Kindergarten, which was far from their home. On her way back one afternoon, a new bus driver stopped and intimated that Raquel had to get off. "Your stop, young lady," he motioned with his hand for her to go ahead; it was her stop.

Raquel looked at him in astonishment, and grabbed hold of her bag and held on to it tightly. "Am not. It's not my stop. Am not."

The driver hesitated at first, and then raised his voice a bit, to show her that now was the time to follow orders. "You have to get off here, young lady. What's your name?" He took the clipboard and ran his finger down the list of the names of the kids on the bus, and looked up.

"Raquel Simone Downing? That you, my dear? Then this is your stop. You have to get off."

Raquel was having none of this, and she shrugged and flatly refused. Traffic congested behind the bus. The driver had to get back on the road to park behind the supermarket before he could negotiate with Raquel.

It took more than half an hour before Raquel mentioned to the driver that her Mommy and Daddy were waiting for her at the Acropolis Garden Store. It was next to the bus stop, she explained. That was when the driver coughed drily and rechecked his schedule.

"The garden store with the green roof? Next to the dry cleaners with the parking lot that bordered the railroad track at the back of Sam's Self-Help," he sounded as if he was now feeling some panic.

Raquel nodded with a small frown on her forehead. "Yes. I told you. I did!"

The driver looked sheepish as he turned the big yellow coach back into Main Road and indicated a sharp left. When the bus pulled into the stop at the Garden Store, a patrol car with two officers were already there talking to her parents. Everyone seemed very relieved when the bus pulled in, but first, the driver had a lot of explaining to do.

For a while, it seemed like tough going, but finally, Raquel heard her Dad guffaw, and everyone relaxed, even the patrolmen.

"She said that did she?" my Dad's voice boomed with pride. "That's my Raquel. Nothing typical about that girl. When you tell her what to do, she listens, man, she really listens. And she does precisely what she's told."

"There was a sense of vindication, a sense of forlorn hope in my Dad's voice. Even though I was still a toddler, Dad looked like an old man to me even then. Pain makes you grow weary and old," Raquel explains somberly over a cup of tea.

"We were very close," Raquel adds, looking up from her hot brew. Every day, when her Dad came home from work, he would slip into her room where she huddled over her books, and they would go over her homework.

Once, when Raquel got stuck on a particular mathematic method, her Dad kept going over and over again until she had it down to a tee. Raquel's Dad, the strong, silent, and insightful one, knew that confidence for a young girl was the golden nectar, the way to the world.

In his gentle manner, he invested her with more confidence than she needed. This was his lasting gift to her: because he believed in her, she believed in her.

Her Dad taught her to protest, to fight, and to stake her claim. Years ago, her Dad brought her a pack of loose-leaf paper for school, and to Raquel's horror, the package was faulty - it contained only half the number of the sheets her Dad paid for.

Her Dad just smiled and asked Raquel what she intended to do about it. Raquel thought for a bit, and then answered: she was going to write to the manufacturers about it. The manufacturers quickly responded. In their first letter, they admitted that the pack did not contain the number of sheets advertised. A few days later, complimentary packets of paper were delivered at Raquel's home as an apology for the error and the inconvenience that resulted from it.

CHAPTER 8:

Mentors

Raquel started out working at the tender age of 11yrs old. She would babysit for a few hours of three little girls to read to them and make sure they did their homework. She then saved her money and made sure that she would buy her parents something special for their birthdays and Mother's Day and Father's Day each holiday. Raquel worked for several city agencies throughout her years, where she developed great relationships as the adult was intrigued by her level of demeanor in which they always wanted to continue to follow her as she would continue in life. At the New York City Department of Employment, she reported back to her previous job at every report card in high school; the staff wanted to see how Raquel was continuing her studies along the way.

Inspector General

Before this, she worked under the leadership of Inspector General Kevin T. Smyley. This was one handsome black man. What would she know about someone nice looking at a young age of 15? She respected him. He was smooth, professional, and never thought he was better than anyone, but he was about doing his job to perfection. A great leader and made sure that each employee was presented with the best possible work. This is where Raquel learned and became a better reader, enjoying reading the New York Times. She liked this job. She saw many black women who resembled her, and they had their college degrees and knowledgeable black men. It was a multicultural office, where everyone got along and did their jobs to perfection. It was a professional atmosphere where I was still a minor in high school learning, and these individuals, whether they knew it or not, are part of who she is today. She would always say, "it is essential what adults do around children would have a lasting effect on them. It was a great experience for her that put her in the right direction. It wasn't every day to have a black boss who was the Inspector General for New York City. At the same time, Kevin T. Smyley's father was a General for the United States, and it was undoubtedly huge to have met a General at the tender age of 15 where not only one black man but two father and son that had a phenomenal background. It was already written that this was the direction that Raquel was supposed to go since this experience began at a very young age. She was already surrounded by those who inspected and advocated and served and protected this country.

Commissioner

As the years went by, she worked with William Bair, who was the Commissioner of Highways. Raquel was his secretary. Handsome as ever, he reminded her of Tom Selleck that played in Blue Bloods. They had long talk sessions while she was still in school, and he always encouraged her to continue studies. He was a family man, and he had tremendous golfing picnics with his family; he would invite her to his family picnics, but she never joined him. At that time, still growing and learning, she felt that she was not ready, and at that time, she liked golf, but she was not a huge fan. Mr. Bair made sure that she would be okay, and he introduced her to a woman of human resources that could help her get a permanent job.

During this time, people connected others to those who could assist in getting a great job, but you would have to demonstrate that you could do the job and had the right skills. As the years went by, Raquel would always visit the office to say hello. She was grateful for him, pointing her in the right direction.

Assistant Attorney General

Later in graduate school, professor Lauren Raysor, a black woman Assistant Attorney General to the Attorney General Elliot Spencer. She taught ethics class. Raquel was intrigued by the course, and she became her mentor. Raquel would meet her at the event she invited her to, shared concerns, and the direction she was going in her studies. She wanted her to speak on issues that were a concern at the forum of events. It was Lauren Raysor who saw the advocacy in Raquel as well.

These are the people who were instrumental in Raquel's journey that she would never forget.

CHAPTER 9:

Friendship

Growing up as a child, Raquel's parents taught her that "friends are a dime a dozen." Her Dad would always say, "We don't have any real friends." And truth be told, many people that she considered friends were not really her friends.

Friends are those people that you don't have to call or speak to every day, but when you do, they are always there for you, to talk to you, to cry with you and to encourage you, and most importantly, they are happy for you and wish you well.

As Raquel grew older, she often found that her so-called friends were merely associates of hers. They were acquaintances rather than friends. Also, she has been betrayed once too often.

Loyalty, integrity, and trust define friendship. Friends don't sleep with your partner, a friend never forgets you during festivities, and a true friend will always honor your accomplishments.

Selena

They say that you are doing very well if you can name one friend for every finger on your left hand. She learned that the hard way, and today she is delighted to have a friend called Selena!

As adults, we rarely make new friends, indeed not as we do in school or college. When we reach the "real world," it's as if we leave that part of ourselves behind.

"This is how I met Selena. We just hit it off." Says Raquel.

According to scientists, girls typically use 20,000 words per day in comparison with boys who use no more than 7,000. The reason why girls are so chatty, they say, is because of significantly higher levels of Foxp2-protein.

Be that as it may, Selena and Raquel loved to talk. They never stopped talking. They even spoke simultaneously, often, both rambling on without taking a breath. And no holds barred - they discussed it all, from the most intimate to the absolutely mundane, if it was there, they had to get it out there.

Where Raquel went, there went Selena, and where Selena went, there was Raquel. They never missed a party. The girls were social and verbal and bubbling with a passion for life. To get access to every single party, they appropriated fake IDs and danced the night away.

Despite their zest for life, the girls were trusted absolutely by their parents, and for a good reason. They always - ALWAYS - followed the rules. Their laughter was wild, but they weren't. They were meticulous and punctual and obedient, and they had each other's back. When Raquel was feeling sick, Selena would accompany her to the emergency room, and vice versa.

They would meet always meet at the train station.

Only when Selena saw Raquel's face in the window would she get on the train. It is really pretty amazing how they abided by every rule their parents, all the grown-ups, made. Raquel and Selena followed their directions blindly, without question. Raquel's Dad refused to allow her to get on a train without an onboard conductor, and they never ever disobeyed him. They were really good girls.

Raquel spoke to Selena every day of her life at ten o'clock, sharp, in the morning, every single day. A week or two before Christmas, they had a long emotional talk. They both ended up crying their hearts out. They were bawling over the phone with the tears rolling down their cheeks, sharing their physical ailments, aches, pains, and sorrows.

Before that, they celebrated the stupendous victory in Raquel's lawsuit with the New York School System, which finally ended after more than a decade of continuous struggle. They winged out to Puerto Rico for a girl's weekend - and what a fabulous weekend it was.

It was the day before Christmas, and this never happened before - Selena called her sometimes before nine-thirty. They reminisced about the old days and about the fun they had in Puerto Rico, and they dreamed up exotic destinations they would pursue once they were retired. They remembered the good times, from way back, and the dreams they had as young girls."

"We've come a long way, the two of us," Selena sighed.

"I have to go," I have to take Dad to LaGuardia Airport," I apologized.

"It's my fault, I called early," Selena reciprocated.

"I'll call back as soon as I dropped off, Daddy," I promised.

"Okay. I'm working from home today. Half a day, only," Selena demurred passively.

By the time Raquel returned home, Selena was in the back of an ambulance on her way to the ER. Three weeks later, she passed away. Raquel thinks of her every single day. After thirty years, their conversation was over.

After Selena's funeral, she became even closer friends with her sister Priscilla. For Raquel, Selena sister Priscilla is now her sister, and Selena's daughter Sadie, is like her niece. Between herself and Priscilla, they will always look after. They want her to finish college. Selena always wanted her daughter to succeed, and Raquel and Priscilla will support her and see that she does. Up there, Selena is smiling. She can see that even after she passed away, Raquel was still there for her, and for Sadie.

Octavia

Octavia was another friend from high school: Raquel met Octavia when they shared their first homeroom class in high school, and they have been inseparable ever since. Where Selena was also Raquel's inseparable friend, Octavia and Raquel did everything together; they made sure that they both would apply for various jobs, and they would go to the agency and work temp jobs while in college. They would practice their skills so that they had a chance to get higher-paying jobs. In high school, Raquel motivated Octavia to get up on time so that they would not be late for class. She would meet her at her train station as a motivation tool. Octavia challenged her to improve and reach for the stars. The girls competed in everything they did and motivated each other to excel, albeit the mundane race to see who could type the fastest or the more revered battle to achieve the highest class grades or Grade Point Average (GPA). They kept each other in line and drove each other to excel because they were so much alike. Octavia would always say that because of Raquel's ability to share her allowance and lunch with her taught her how to share with others because of her generosity. To Raquel, that's what friends should do: sharing is caring.

"We were so similar that I saw her more like my sister. Her entire family loves me, I guess, and I am included in all facets of their life, and that includes her siblings and nephews and nieces. They are a massive family." Says Raquel.

From the very start, they were both ambitious, and from early on, they aspired to find jobs. They wanted to earn their own money, and both planned to spend a lot of that money to go to Broadway plays. They loved the theatre, and for many years, they were the youngest girls in attendance.

As life moved on, they remained close despite Octavia's move to California. Regardless of the distance, they spent Thanksgiving together a year ago. Just before Octavia's son graduated from the college Raquel attended, the girls celebrated their friendship by going on a luxury boat cruise.

Time stood still for them. They still compete, and they still love doing things together.

CHAPTER 10:

Pinnacle Moments

⸺⸺⸺⸺⸺⸺ ৶ ૭ ৶ ૭ ⸺⸺⸺⸺⸺⸺

"I have no doubt that my greatest accomplishment is the attainment of self-knowledge. I fully understand who I am as a human being. I know my purpose, and that opened the world for me. It allowed me to go back to school, and it compels me to help anyone in need. Today, I take nothing for granted. Whether I cook, work out, shop, or travel, every day is a gift, and maybe my last. So, while I am alive, anything is possible, and I will never give up. Every dream I ever dreamed can come true - a hundred times. All I have to do is to follow my dreams.

My greatest achievement was being the best parent that I could be.

I had to work two jobs to ensure that my son received a private school education because I wanted the very best for him. My son did well and became a fantastic athlete - all city champion in football and track and field. He was always very determined. I nurtured my son as I was nurtured as a child, but he earned everything I ever gave him. He was an achiever from day one and did very well in school."

Raquel, the little duckling, slowly developed into a swan. As she matured, Raquel became more aloof but also more accomplished. It started with academics. She was spurred on by the tragedy of life. She desperately wanted to delete herself from her parents' radar, so she tried to free them from any needless worries and decided to take care of business all on her own.

She had a perfect 100% attendance record, just for starters, and she quickly became a leader in the Girl Scouts. As a Spelling Bee participant, she took the first prize at her school and went on to represent her school regionally. She wrote well too, and one of her essays brought the coveted Martin Luther King Award home to her proud parents; the commendations poured in. But that was not all! She also became a budding fast track star with a room full of trophies. She was on a roll.

HERITAGE

RAQUEL: "It is my faith, my most profound belief, that my life, my existence has been preordained. My only function is to fulfill my role, to embrace my destiny."

RAQUEL: "My family has always been brilliant-minded people."

The Birth of "Kids are People Too Inc."

Her Mom cared for many of the kids in the neighborhood and cooked and fed everyone hungry every single day. In later years, Raquel continued this tradition and even took it to another level - one of her first start-ups was 'Kids are People Too Inc.' She partnered with her Mom, and they both taught the toddlers while her son took care of the day-to-day management. It provided an extraordinary opportunity for the mother and daughter to share their love for children. At the same time, her son learned how to start and manage a small business and generate and manage cash flow.

CHAPTER 11:

But I'm Proud of Harvard!

"Everything changed when I went back to school. And now, with me at Harvard, I encounter some resentment. Some of my friends stopped calling. Some won't even greet me in the street. I would like to believe that they are just a bit jealous, a bit envious - but if they really knew me, they would know I am still the same person. I always had a drive; I always had goals." Says Raquel.

She smiles again, looks down, and goes on.

"I am proud of Harvard, of course, I am, so don't get me wrong - but I am nevertheless still a woman and a loving person. I can hang out with anybody. I don't judge someone's resume before I hang out with them. But I won't tolerate disrespect nor disloyalty. If you do not respect my friendship and consortium, you cannot be my friend. Education did not change me even a little bit. I get along with everybody, but I won't back down when someone offends me."

As a black woman, I am very proud of my accomplishments, but it has not been easy. I do what I do because it's ordained for me to be this person. I do not try to fit in anyone's world; nevertheless, it comes with struggle and pain. Going back to school for me has been very lonely. There were days that I felt like giving up and saying forget about it. Although it was ordained somehow, I thought I would have had a stronger support system, but I didn't; the people I thought I could depend on turned on me and drifted. I will never forget when I learned that I was accepted into Harvard Medical School; somehow, the acceptance letter went into the spam folder. I received a telephone call from the university. I needed to report to London two days after receiving the call. This was an international program. It went like this.

We are reaching out to inform you that you have been accepted, and we sent a letter to you a while ago, and you never responded. If you are still interested, you need to be in London on Saturday. My response was that's in two days. How can this be possible? I got off the telephone and began trying to figure out how can I make this happen. I had no money, I never been to London, and it wasn't one of the places on my bucket list. How am I going to pay for this tuition, and how am I going to afford London. I had no one to call for help. I had the exact amount to book a hotel and airplane package and, of course, prayer to cover and protect me in my travels outside the country with no money.

After all, I stepped out on faith, the little voice that told me to apply for this program, and indeed I got accepted. I didn't know anything about London, and what a surprise I had made arrangements and whined up staying in the area the world of the princess in Kensington Palace and Gardens. When I got there I was already nervous. I wonder how will I fit in. Although, in the white world, I might be respected. However, I'm still seen as a threat. I don't get the juicy scholarships or the friendly assistance provided to my counterparts who are foreigners and come from all over the white world.

Also, though I might be in their world, I am not from their world. One of the very well-known professors at Harvard mocked my accent. He was quite rude as a matter of fact, and he made crude jokes about how ethnic my dialect was. He could not understand "black" and ridiculed me before my peers.

To my astonishment, when he spoke to a woman from Hungary afterward - she could barely speak English - he handled her with empathy and thoughtfulness. He would never even think about mocking her accent or dialect.

He nevertheless told our class that when he was a boy growing up in Brooklyn, his mother's boss told her to move out of Brooklyn if she ever wanted him to be successful. "You need to move to an area where his accent can change," the so-called boss explained to his mother.

I could not let it go. "First off, I am not from Brooklyn. I come from Cambria Heights in Queens, and I spent my summers in Sag Harbor," I said, "and as a matter of fact, your dialect, sir, sounds precisely like many of my uncles.

His apology was hollow, of course. You cannot apologize for the comments you actually meant at the time.

"Was that more like an isolated incident?" I questioned her gingerly. She seemed thoughtful and then chuckled. "I don't think so. During our presentations last month at Harvard Med, I was bombarded with question after question. Still, nobody asked questions when the "white" students did their presentations."

"How do you know that was racist? Maybe they were just more interested and more stimulated by your presentation?" I added.

She looked at me and nodded. "That might very well be the case. I did get rave reviews, much more than anybody else. Although, the same Harvard Director belittled me in the eyes of a group of Harvard Medical School staff later on. They were out to get me. At least, that's what I thought.

They were waiting, waiting for me to screw up - if I failed to do the work, or misunderstood or misspoke, they were ready and waiting. But they couldn't, and they didn't. What they did not anticipate from the "black woman" who penetrated their serene white space were brains. I am very bright. I was accepted into the program on merit - no special favors and no affirmative action. My intelligence caught them by surprise.

"So, you think they were prejudiced against you being African American and all?" I pressed her more.

"No. It was my classmates, my white peers, who felt that I was poorly treated. They came to me - up in arms."

"It was unfair. Their questions were ridiculous." They were embarrassed. From my point of view, I think I surprised the Harvard establishment very much. I had a highly sophisticated concept, and that was beyond their expectations for a "funny talking black woman." So, they acted out when I required nothing from them. They expected to have to carry me, and I expected them to underestimate me. That does not mean I wasn't profoundly hurt, though. I was. I am. I have a terrible sense of sadness in my heart over this incident."

"Will you report it - try to get some sort of justice from Harvard?" I asked in a whisper.

She thought for half a minute. "No. I am not surprise. This is the world that we live in that must change. Then, maybe."

CHAPTER 12:

A Flawed System

"It was never my dream to teach. For me, teaching was a means to an end. Education allowed me to actively raise my son and pursue a career at the same time. The money was adequate, and above all, I had time. I could be there for my son and provide him with stability and a resemblance to family life. We were happy as well, and that counts for something.

We had a working routine. I picked him up from school every day. When we arrived at home, I would start cooking, and he would do his homework. We prayed all the time, and always before every meal. We were really grateful for what we had.

After dinner, I sat down with him, and we went over his homework together to make sure that he was on point and did not require any help. Together, we created a perfect little world. And while he became an outstanding student, I became a really great teacher - if I can say so myself.

As he grew up, I considered joining the military. I was always keen on the military, and I believed that it would be good for me and great for my son.

I had enough qualifications to join as an officer. Still, we hit a snag: they refused to accept me as an officer. It was a deal-breaker. The recruiter wanted me to start at a grade E6. The recruiter didn't know that my Dad was a veteran who informed me and explained to me that with my qualifications, I could sign up as an officer. If I did not become an officer, I would be paid less. I already had two master's degrees. I knew then that I couldn't sign up.

In the end, my son joined the military, and believe me, I supported his choice vehemently. It all worked out in the end.

But that wasn't just it. I knew that just being a teacher wasn't enough. Before entering the school system, I was a manager. So, I continued to pursue studies in education administration. From past experience, I already knew how to manage a facility, supervising staff. So, this shouldn't be difficult running a school building. I already knew how flawed the system was. I was qualified. I was asked to participate in countless interviews for positions within the Department of Education. I applied to well over 100 positions. I received letters from everywhere about how impressive my background was, and yet no one would hire me. Finally, I became an administrator, and there I was."

Ms. Prose

Ms. ProSe is the name I received at court by Judge Lewis while trying to make a system wrong be right. I sort out filing an RJI against the largest school system in the country to clear my name. I was alone in this world that almost took my life away. I never gave up. I was determined to clear this up even if it meant that I would lose everything, but I will never let my name be tarnished. A system that I played chess while they continued to play checkers.

The object for me was to strategically figure out who the players were and how to knock them down one by one. I was under attack at all times; that's when I realized what I was doing was for the good of myself and my son. I had to show him that no matter what the obstacles are, you must fight to the end.

There were many opponents while fighting the DOE, and I had no friends, and I lost almost everything, but I never gave up. I am talking about my name, my reputation, and my integrity as they were at stake.

I can finally take care of my child and send him to college, which was approaching while I had no healthcare-which is paramount. There was no way that I could allow the DOE to manipulate the system to get away with murdering me. Yes, it was murder trying to subterfuge a system, trying to cover up what was happening and getting rid of me for no reason other than doing the job correctly, while staying in compliant. Not to mention, I applied for jobs with all experiences and credentials I had, but I could not get a job. Jobs were offering me $10 an hour. My reputation was tarnished. I had nobody. I had no one. I couldn't tell my family I was embarrassed. I always worked hard for everything. I worked with so many great businesses and developed experiences that many wished they had, and just at a snap of a finger, I was erased.

The Court was in shock when they read my briefs and exhibits. This was a wakeup call for the Supreme Court that something was wrong. Justice Lewis was the first judge in the case. She clearly asked corporation counsel to have someone from the NYCDOE to appear in court. She wanted to know how could this woman with a mathematical background with all this experience and knowing math could be out of a job.

Every time I appeared in court, they never showed up. The NYCDOE lawyer came to court while he was not prepared and wanted briefs from me, and yet he could not get themselves in line. Corporation counsel thought that this would be a slammed dunk, but they never checked my jacket and did not know that I had always been a person that would never sit down but always stood up even under an attack.

Nervous I was since I was fighting a large system, and I was representing myself ProSe, so this was huge. Judge Lewis recused herself, and so did others. They were able to see the injustice right before their eyes and did not want to be a part of this reckless system. It was Judge Bloom who overturned every win I had. That's when I knew what was wrong there. The judge became red when on the record, I asked him to recuse himself because he was biased. The entire court was in shock. Lawyers in the court thought I was an attorney and realized that I was representing myself. The entire court filled to its capacity, being flabbergasted. The judge asked me to get an attorney.

I explained that a judge is supposed to review both sides and follow the law. Our court system is the reason so many people are in jail right now. I am an educator, and I have taught many students over these years to become doctors, lawyers, and or judges.

CHAPTER 13

Article 78 to Rubber Room

I commenced a lawsuit against the NYCDOE. Article 78 was what I had to file in the NYS Supreme court. It was two days before the New Year was about to begin. I only had the exact amount to file an article 78. It was the worst experience of my life. I almost lost my home, and I had no money to pay utility bills at home.

> *"The worst experience in my life - ever. Never again! I won't survive something like this ever again." Who could have known that God would have me sue the NYC Department of Education?*

"Yes, they placed me in the rubber room for doing my job correctly. I never knew that the school system had created an in-house prison for educators they wanted isolated and removed from teaching. Then I became an inmate myself. They forced me into the rubber room where

I was forced to sit there in the capacity as an administrator for three and a half years sentence.

As a result of suing them and getting the matter overturned with a win, I was sent to the rubber room as punishment. This forced me to take a stand. And I did. I sued the New York City Department of Education - one of the most powerful institutions in the United States. I had no money and no representation. I had to appear ProSe, so the court called me Mrs. ProSe. How ironic is that? And the State brought big guns into court, some of the most respected and revered law firms with unlimited resources and enough lawyers to fill a school bus.

I sued them four times and won every time.

It started when a student was supposed to go on a school trip, and the teacher decided to leave him at a bodega store. The student was hit by a truck, and the parent reported the matter in another district.

The NYCDOE tried to sweep the matter under the carpet. Still, the superintendent in the other district contacted the school where I worked, and I was tasked to investigate the matter.

As a result, most of those involved, including the superintendent, were fired or forced into early retirement. So, I suddenly became the face of the matter, and the

NYCDOE simply discontinued my services as the Assistant Principal despite the fact that I had an exemplary record.

I fought them for a decade - all the way to the Supreme court. Several Judges recused themselves; meanwhile, the NYCDOE canvassed to find a judge partial to their cause. I asked the Judge to recuse himself because he was not impartial. He clearly favored the City instead of judging the matter based on Law. It took ten years to go through the court system, which is longer than a murder trial takes. The case eventually went to the appellate division, where it was overturned in my favor.

I always represent myself.

I became very eager to learn the Law and attended Brooklyn College. I enrolled in their Paralegal program over weekends. That is where I learned how to prepare briefs.

Of course, I did ask my cousin Belinda, an attorney. She reviewed my documents. It was a long journey, but I had to clear my name and escape the rubber-room.

The way the Department treated me was shocking.

The Rubber room made headlines, while many before me made a lot of noise. Many of the victims of the rubber room lost their jobs, and it caused the deaths of many. Dead Man Walking! That's what they would say the minute a new member enter the Rubber room. The system was designed to impoverish these teachers and administrators, but many of them did nothing wrong. Some were in for time and attendance, sexual battery, and some for driving while intoxicated. The rubber room was a prison, but the inmates went home at night.

One hundred and fifty people were crammed into the rubber room. I was in shock. Some people came to work in pajamas. I could not believe that this was actually going on. People were sleeping stretched out on beach chairs. Sometimes, couples made babies in there. And there were many fights. Every day, before 8.30 in the morning, things would go wrong. But for the Grace of God, I would not have survived this.

I was broke and had no healthcare. I could not provide for my family. That all changed when I started, "Kids are People Too." I even managed to save some money, and I succeeded in keeping my home.

I wrote to the governor and all the banks, and I wrote many letters about the actions of the mortgage lender who wanted to foreclose without granting me the opportunity to modify my mortgage. I even appointed a lawyer who was thrilled and a little surprised that I succeeded in securing a modification loan at a two percent interest rate. After many years in foreclosure, I was financially healthy again.

I was mistreated, and the facts were misrepresented. It was a scam used to get rid of someone who "rocked the boat." It is all part of the public record now.

In the end, the court decided in my favor. Still, it took ten years of my life and resulted in financial and emotional hardships. But in the end, God's hand protected us, and we did not lose our home.

The system that was supposed to put the children first failed. The children counted for nothing. And I stood up against that. If I cowered before them and buckled under pressure, I would not have been who I am today. Nor my son, I believe. So, it ended well, and yes, today, I am a retired administrator and educator from New York City Department of Education.

> "In one sense, I was broken; in another sense, I was reborn. I wanted something new, something different. I wanted to go back to school. And here I am, on my way to become a medical educator, biomedicine informatics, and an ethicist doctor. At the moment, I am doing an Informatics biomedical course at Harvard Medical School. I face a long road ahead, but I am happy, and I am doing brilliantly."

CHAPTER 14:

Just Raquel!

Raquel Downing is genuinely a native New Yorker, and her roots run deep down to the core of New York culture. Her cousin, Al Downing, played for the Yankee. He was the pitcher when Hammering Hank Aaron made baseball history.

Raquel is an all-rounder. She worked in various fields and studied and graduated with multiple degrees from the great universities, including Harvard.

She is presently attending two medical schools where she will complete her doctorate studies in Biomedicine Ethics and Integrative Medicine.

She is a successful entrepreneur with businesses as diverse as childcare and vending machines in the breast cancer health field. Also, she is an athlete and a salsa dancer; she attends boxing classes and enjoys sports; she learned how to play the piano at a young age; she used to be a girl scout. Her son is an all-star running back, a special forces soldier, hero, and veteran, who now works as a manager for a Fortune 500 company and completing his MBA degree.

But that is just her story, not who she is.

It started the first day after I arrived at the school. Who could have imagined that it would end as Downing vs. the NYCDOE?

I remember studying segregation Brown vs. the Board of Education when I was in high school. Back then, Blacks were not provided with an education equal to the education Whites received. Working in the school system, I believed it was a privilege to provide the best that I could possibly offer to everyone. At "222," I was the only woman on the cabinet team.

If sexual harassment were taken seriously, many of the administration and teachers would have lost their jobs. But the system did not care. Do nothing and see what happens until the parents come knocking. I was so naïve at the time, but I knew it was a problem. Every single day I went home, I took my job with me. It was a horrible system.

A white male teacher exposed his pierced nipples to the girls in his class. The girls were upset and complained to me. I reported their allegations to my superior, but instead of reprimanding the teacher, the students were merely removed from his class. This made the impact on the girls a lot worse. The teacher violated them, but they got punished. For them, this might very well be the beginning of a dysfunctional relationship with the opposite sex. Because the teacher was white and the children were black and Latino, nothing happened.

One of the men, a special needs teacher, targeted a young girl in his class. It began with inappropriate questions about her menstrual cycle. According to the girl, the teacher often cornered her in class, and she and her mother often complained. After reaching a dead-end with the school authorities, the parents reported the teacher's conduct to the police. As a result, the school turned on the girl, and her parents had to remove her from the school.

It was my job to get involved, and as a result, I simply became a target too. Some of the guidance counselors manipulated students and got them to write inappropriate and untrue allegations about my conduct in the restroom. I was flabbergasted and could not fathom how the children survived such a vile and dysfunctional school system that employed so many very sick people.

I was banished to the basement of the school. I oversaw the entire special education department - mathematics, social studies, graduation, and so on. One day a custodian of the school took me down to the dungeons to retrieve a specific Individualized Education Plan. The basement was where it all started for me. It was filled with records going back more than twenty years. It was actually quite unbelievable.

I just could not understand why these records were stored in the school's basement rather than following the students as they progressed through the school system after middle school.

What astonished me more was when I started going through the records. I noticed soon enough that the majority of the students with special needs never received the attention and services they were not only entitled to but dependent upon in terms of their IEP.

The "evidence" was hidden in the basement where it remained hidden until I stumbled upon it. The ramifications stunned me. I had no doubt that many of these forgotten and ignored children ended up incarcerated without any comprehension of their condition, and without any coping skills, any understanding of how to deal with their emotions, albeit that they suffered from speech delays, emotional disturbances, or post-trauma.

Our school lacked real leadership, and as a result, never did the right thing for the children in our care - ever. And things gradually deteriorated. Books for the new school year were routinely sourced from the friends of insiders, Kick-backs were regularly paid. Corruption was rife. So, I spoke out, and I became a target.

Word was out: I expected a lot more for our Black and Latino children; they deserved a much better education. So, I sued the Department of Education - and I won.

The Department went ballistic after that. From that moment on, they refused to keep me on their payroll. I remember sitting in a conference room at the regional office. The superintendent and her flunkies were all involved in conference-calls. I was supposed to look up to them, and they simply could not understand how a black woman could remain so unintimidated by them.

Education had become all about who you knew, not what you knew. It was only about networking. If you were an insider, your sons and daughters were given tenure with top salaries even when they were totally inexperienced and came straight from college. Blacks rarely made it into these clicks. We were all still living in a world of Brown vs. Board of Education. Segregation of schools remains unconstitutional even if all schools were perfectly equal.

No one really cared about anything at all once the point system used to reward staff and purchase supplies for the school was converted into actual dollars. And I unearthed even more evidence of thievery as things went along. I simply could not comprehend how the Department could allow inexperienced administrators to run the budget without any expert-control whatsoever. The system was designed to make it effortless to steal money from the top down. Schools would create after-school programs as spontaneously as any student could figure out how to tie their shoelaces.

It defies logic. If students were not coming to class or learning during the school day, why would they engage in an after-school program? The explanation was obvious. It was designed to enrich administrators and teachers to increase their pensions, to buy homes, and so on.

Meanwhile, a lot of students left and moved on and were lost. I am sure many are still struggling if they are not dead or in jail. It was a domino effect. Most of the parents did not know how to fight for their children, and many were intimidated.

I was later sent to a school, "PS 999." It had a principal who was very nasty to her staff, children, and parents. I was amazed at how she treated the team; it was as if the United States was a third-world country.

Fortunately for her, she was Dominican, but she nevertheless thought she was better than her staff, most of whom were from there too. She belittled them because many did not have citizenship, and she held it over their heads. I remember the superintendent, who sent me over. She and her cronies knew this woman as a nasty piece of work, and they relished how I would finally be put in my place.

This was typical of the street-fighter mentality in the school system. I often listened as the nasty woman called her staff "dumb." I found it hard to believe and even harder to understand. Luckily for her, she never tried this approach with me until much later. When she did, I simply informed her that I was out of her league. She exploded, yelled, screamed, and cried like a newborn baby when I refused to kneel before her and never allowed her to address me in a rude or deprecating manner. I couldn't believe that this was a school with a Principal behaving in this manner.

I was subsequently sent to another school, and the new principal was very rude as well. She knew me before I went there, but I quickly understood that she was one of them, just like the rest of the bullies I encountered so far. I thought she would have been a better person; after all, she was once demoted and somehow gained her position back.

The manipulators at the top sent her to another school with the explicit belief that she would destroy it, which suited their plans. Rumors circulated that she would put Vaseline on her face and sweats to fight her staff.

After completion of her destructive mission, her new school had merely fifty students left. Still, according to the NYDOE, this was a job well-done, and she retained her status as a School Principal.

I was taking the NYCDOE head-on now. I filed multiple cases based on human rights violations against them to make the world aware of what was happening under their noses.

They fought a war and never kept the contest locked down in court. They played by their own rules, and despite my perfect record of tax compliance, I was suddenly audited by a quite antagonistic woman looking for discrepancies of any kind. The NYCDOE sent in-house investigators to my home, and this only ended when I attempted to get a court order against them. The investigator was eventually dismissed as a result of this.

The head of the Department of HR became obsessed with me. As an attorney herself, she was perplexed that I kept winning in the courts. Infatuated, she would call everywhere I went to find out what I was doing and what I was wearing. Everyone knew it was wrong, but they were too scared to do anything out of fear of losing their jobs.

After another victory, I was sent to yet another school. At times, the NYCDOE would appoint black counsel and send black liaison officers along to disavow any appearance of racial discrimination. One of them was Sebastian. He appeared to be kind and honest, but he was very slick at the same time.

He bamboozled the school system out of at least 25,000 dollars in extra payments for overtime over the years. He was subsequently forced to resign. And apart from his dishonesty, he was conceited too - you could not tell him anything.

During his investigation, he placed the students under his charge in the "jail-system" he created at his school, and he used the safe-room to incarcerate the children for nearly anything they did. I explained to him that he was institutionalizing the children and that this will perpetuate their behavioral pattern, without any reaction from him. I knew that the system he created replicated the unwanted behavior in the children. How amazing that he became an employee of the union after all of this.

I remember one time getting a letter from the union lawyer that told me to let sleeping dogs lie.

Are you serious!

This was not a union that supported all their members; they supported their friends only. I was not friends with any of them. Other Unions had to dance in tune with the City when he spoke to the members. My Dad was a lifetime union member. He never gave in and always spoke on behalf of all of its members. His example allowed me to persistently fight for my job and my self-respect until I was victorious at the very end.

To come even closer to understanding this remarkable woman, we need to go to her when she was a young woman who studied nursing. During a nursing mathematics class, the professor wrote a math problem on the blackboard. The students had to solve it. Most of the students followed the suggested method. They managed to solve the problem, but one student, a woman named Raquel Simone Downing, developed a brand-new approach to solving the equation.

This seemed to infuriate the professor, who demanded that she explained her method to him before she explained it to the entire class. The young Raquel did not back off and defended her approach. Mathematics is a vast subject, and there are many, many valid roads you can take in pursuit of a solution.

Raquel went on to become a beloved high school mathematics teacher, and she was eventually invited by Fordham University to join their Ph.D. program in mathematics. It was a tremendous honor, but there was just one snag. Board of Education was a corrupt and inefficient organization that operated at a level of pettiness that is hard to believe. Her supervisor simply refused to sign off on Raquel's participation in the program. This cost

Raquel a Ph.D. in mathematics that Fordham would have subsidized 100%. Raquel was the only woman in the Math Department, and she faced an uphill battle.

One woman changed the course of her life. She was Ms. London, a native of Jamaica - a woman with poise, style, and a brilliant mind. Under her mentorship, Raquel's mathematical skills developed beyond belief, especially in the field of manipulatives, which brought mathematics to life and lit up her mind.

It took only one brilliant woman to free the mind of another intelligent woman. Ms. London recognized Raquel's potential and helped her to unleash her spirit and expand her mind. Raquel is a survivor and a winner, and her story is the story of every woman. Her trials and triumphs and hardship and pain are familiar to every woman in the world.

Someone once told Raquel, who was anxious about an upcoming interview: "Child, what's for you will be for you." Raquel was so moved by her words that she still insists today that it changed her life. The woman, it turned out, was the famous American poet, singer, writer, and activist, Maya Angelou. Raquel left her with a new sense of hope and an autograph for her son.

"What's for me will be for me no matter what. Granted, it might take me a bit longer to get there, but every step I take brings me closer to my goal."

"Thank you for your service." That's all they said after all my years of serving the children in the school system. On top of it all, I just left the hospital after almost dying from complications. The school system put me through a lot after being in and out of the hospital for past years. By the time I left the hospital the last time, I was so fragile as if I was on my death bed."

"We understand that you have been through a lot. In two days, we will let you know whether you can retire. What will you do now - once you get well?"

"I had no idea what to say. I sat there, trying to talk, but I just left the hospital, and I had no idea what comes next."

Then they said something else. "We believe there is no doubt in our minds that you will do something special, something great, as soon as you recover, as soon as you are healthy again."

So, what then is the point of the Raquel Simone Downing story?

Ms. London and Maya Angelou are the points of the story. It took these women a few minutes to change Raquel's life and the life of her son forever. And that is why

Raquel's story is so important. A whole new generation of women is desperate for role models that can give them hope and inspire them to be more and better. That is why Raquel's story is so important. Insubordinate, Raquel was not. Being obedient to do right for others is what Raquel has always fought to do and what's necessary.